THaT'S JUST Me!

written by
Shannon Jones

illustrated by
Melissa Bailey

This book is dedicated to Kendal and Louis.
You are beautifully and wonderfully made both on the inside and out!
Mom and dad love you!
To my mommy and daddy,
Thank you for always supporting me and providing a platform for my
creativity to shape the person I am and continue to become!

Emma
has spirally golden locks of hair.

Mike
has red spiky hair.

I have curly coils of brown hair
and that's just me!

Courtney's eyes are twinkling blue
as the stars in the sky.

Kayla's eyes are green
like fresh peas.

My eyes are chestnut brown
and round like a coffee bean
and that's just me!

Patrick's skin
is the complexion
of sweet Georgia peaches.

Haron's skin is dark brown
like warm fudge brownies.

My skin is golden brown
like honey from a beehive
and that's just me!

Louis' nose is long
like the prickly strings on a violin.

Lindsey's nose is narrow
like a winding river.

My nose is broad
like a baby chick's beak
and that's just me!

The world is
a melting pot filled with
beautiful people.
No one person is the same.
Every person is unique
and that is why
I LOVE ME!

CPSIA information can be obtained
at www.ICGtesting.com
Printed in the USA
LVOW01s1749101115
461856LV00010B/12/P